All Tangled Up

A Rose Prairie Story
Sierra Shipley

I0619279

Books By Sierra

The Claiming Her Series
His Temptation
His Disaster
His Reward
His Challenge
Interconnected Stand Alones
Yes, Captain
Hey, Neighbor
The Single Dads Club
Loved by the Single Dad
Nanny for the Single Dad
Desired by the Single Dad

SIERRA SHIPLEY

For those of us who always dreamt of
walking through Christmas lights with someone special.
This is for us.

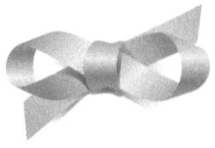

Prologue

Rose Prairie City Council Meeting
November
Sammie

Bang! The gavel pounding on the table is sweet music to my ears.

"The votes are unanimous. Miss Samantha Williams will be the new Rose Prairie Event Coordinator." Pride wells in my chest as Mayor Desmond addresses the underwhelming crowd—the average age being sixty-five. The large, balding man nods his head toward me in acknowledgment. "We wish you the best of luck and look forward to seeing how you transform our town square. I'm sure it will be a Christmas Spectacular to remember." Faint clapping is sprinkled throughout the room as the mayor drones on. "Next on the agenda…"

The rest of the meeting fades into the background while my insides swirl.

I've done it. Look out world! Here comes Sammie Williams. Nothing can stop me now.

An overwhelming sense of accomplishment and joy threatens tears that in *no way* need to be seen by anyone else.

It's long been a dream of mine to create a festive Christmas in a small town like Rose Prairie. City life is no place for me, always longing for a tiny town somewhere off in the middle of nowhere. Leaving Chicago behind has been one of the best decisions I've ever made.

And now I get to do what I've always wanted.

The City Council has just announced *me* as their new event coordinator. I'm honestly still in shock. I mean, my proposal was elaborate and well thought out that it'd almost seem impossible for them to *not* pick me. The proposal was made several weeks ago in front of this very council and called for a complete overhaul. Toss out the old and outdated Christmas decorations for the town square and revamp with one-of-a-kind attractions. They said, and I quote, "We need some young blood in this town" and boy did they find that with me.

Silently, I vow to do everything in my power to make Rose Prairie the go-to destination for Christmas in small town USA.

Chapter One

Sammie

Wandering through the warehouse where the city stores its holiday decorations is eerie. Buzzing overhead lights, the echoing of every step, the smell of mildew tainting the air. Not to mention the creepy oversize Santa Claus that definitely contains lead paint and has a smile pulled straight from a nightmare.

"I'm thinking this needs to go." Pointing at the Santa from hell, I continue walking down the aisle. Quinn peels off blue painter's tape, gingerly placing an X on Santa's nose. She's a student at Rosewood College in town and needed a job. It just so happened that I needed an assistant. She also might have been the only one to respond to the ad I posted in the coffee shop, but that's neither here nor there. She's been a great help getting things organized.

Quinn leans back, pushing up the bridge of her glasses, whistling as she glances around. "Wow. This place is something else. How old is this stuff anyway? And why haven't they replaced them yet?" Quinn is a blond, quirky, nerdy type of girl. Her most defining feature aside from the glasses that constantly slide down the bridge of her nose, is her short stature. Myself being of average height, Quinn seems tiny compared to me. Sometimes I wonder if she was a gymnast with how tiny she is.

"All valid questions," I sigh. Bending down and tucking my long dark hair behind my ear, I examine a giant box of what looks to be garland, the green dye faded into an off-looking blue. "From what I heard, the last mayor had a sentimental attachment to all this." Nudging the box with my booted toe, Quinn peels off more tape to mark things to be discarded. "Her grandmother's grandmother or whoever started the Christmas Spectacular event, so all this junk was kept around."

"Then I'd say it's good that you were chosen for the job. This shi- stuff is terrible." Having worked with Quinn for several weeks, it's clear that this girl isn't used to censoring herself. Not that I mind, but she's trying so hard that I have to chuckle. "It's amazing they don't frighten any children that show up."

The image of Kevin McCallister screaming and running away, arms flailing comes to mind. "I'm sure they do," I snicker. "This stuff even scares me," I admit. "Just look at this nativity. Their poor faces are completely gone. And Joseph has no hands." Quinn and I both laugh at the disfigured plastic figure. How just his hands are missing is beyond me, but the sight of a faceless, handless Joseph is hilarious.

After an hour of walking through the warehouse and placing Xs on almost everything, we've only managed to find hanging snowflakes that need some TLC and they'll be presentable. Everything else: lights, trees, lamp post decorations, Santa and his sleigh, Frosty and friends, and the gingerbread houses are unsalvageable. It seems like a waste of time, considering my whole proposal was to get rid of everything, but at least I can tell the council that we saved what we could. I'm not trying to come in and throw away over a hundred years of tradition, but it's time to move into the twenty-first century. It's better to have them on my side instead of against me. They can think what they want, all I'm trying to do is make this town a showstopper.

Growing up watching all the Hallmark movies built somewhat of an obsession in me. So much so, that when I had the opportunity, I left the city for the smallest, most picturesque town I could find smack in the middle of nowhere. My cousin Mel teases that I'm only out here looking for my small-town romance, but that's not the only reason. It's just one of many.

Who doesn't love a small town romance?

The real pull towards simple town life is Christmas. In my opinion, no one does Christmas better than a small town. Along with the glimmering lights, it brings out a time of peace and joy. Christmas spirit is a real thing and I will argue that until the day I die. Watching those movies and seeing the decorations transform a drab town into a fairytale has always astounded me. A simple town square can suddenly become a hub of beauty and magic.

Sure, I romanticize Christmas, but it truly is a magical time. Bundling up in coats and sweaters. Baking mouth watering cookies. Exchanging thoughtful gifts. Spending time with loved ones. But the best of all: the Christmas lights. That sense of wonder and beauty that's given by such a simple thing. There's no other way to put it.

It's magic.

Magic might have to be what helps me pull off this Christmas Spectacular. I only have three weeks until everything is unveiled. Keeping with tradition, every Christmas Eve the town holds what they call the Christmas Spectacular. Hundreds of townspeople gather together in the dark of Christmas Eve to see the lights glow. The whole town gets involved; hot chocolate stands, carriage rides, the annual Chili cookoff, and the local bakery sets up a sweets shop. I moved here just before Christmas last year and fell in love with this town. But looking around, I knew I could do better. Now here I am with only weeks to prepare and barely any materials to work with. Silently, I curse the woman who stepped down from my new position a month before Christmas.

What in the world are you doing?

The first night officially on the job is spent scouring the internet to find replacement items for all the ones we threw out. What kind of town doesn't decorate *before* Christmas?

It seems like every year Christmas decorations come out earlier and earlier. One minute it's Halloween and by midnight—boom—Christmas. Not that I'm complaining. Personally, I think it should be Christmas all-year around, but this town has its way of doing things. Small towns tend to move at their own pace, even if a snail could outrun it, and this one is no exception.

The eggnog and brandy concoction slowly works to ease the tension in my shoulders that has set in. My luck, as it turns out, seems to have vanished with getting the job. First, most of the stuff needs to be tossed. Second, they are only giving me three weeks to overhaul the decorations—and believe me, I tried to get them to let me start sooner. Thirdly, there are no viable options for replacements. None. I've looked everywhere. Even trusty old marketplace is a dud. The only thing I can think to do to fulfill my vision is to make things myself.

ALL TANGLED UP

Uncle John, my dad's brother, taught me when I was younger how to work with my hands. He's a handyman and constantly has his fingers covered in grease, but he made sure my cousins and I knew the basics around power tools. Many days after school were spent in his shop "helping" with jobs. We'd make wooden guns that shoot rubber bands or put together wooden stools. Some of my best childhood memories come from that shop.

I'll make everything by hand if I have to. Nothing is going to stop me from completing this project.

. . ✦ . .

"NEXT, WE HAVE MISS Samantha Williams sharing her preparations for the Christmas Spectacular."

All evening I waited my turn to address the city council at their bi-weekly meeting. Wiping my hands down my thighs, I stand and make my way up to the podium. As the Event Coordinator, I'm expected to be present for every meeting as well as report on the progress being made. At the last meeting, they gave me permission to evaluate the warehouse and do what I deemed best. Tonight though, I have a sense that things aren't going to go smoothly.

Clearing my throat, the feedback of the microphone screeches, causing everyone to jump and cover their ears. "Let's try this again," I joke, smiling broadly at the group sitting before me. "My assistant and I went to the warehouse and looked at all the decorations stored there." I pause, making sure to make eye contact with the members before continuing. "Unfortunately, most of the equipment was beyond repair.

Many items were broken, discolored, or a safety hazard-" before I can continue, a shrill voice interrupts me.

"Now, hold on there Miss Williams." The urge to roll my eyes is almost overwhelming as Mrs. Lori Haverford stands from her seat at the table before me. "What do you mean a safety hazard? Those items are part of the tradition of this town. Yet you describe them as trash." Her words are full of disbelief and outrage. However, I'm not surprised. The vote for me to be the new coordinator may have been unanimous, but Lori Haverford is a born and bred Rose Prairie native. She comes from a long line of proud Rosies —as they call themselves—and is the only one who gave pushback on my proposal.

Deep, calm breaths Sammie.

Forcing a gentle smile, I respond. "Yes, unfortunately. Quinn and I did a very thorough inspection of the items, many of which contained lead paint that was flaking off. Some objects were broken and had sharp edges that could harm anyone walking by. Not to mention the mildew that was covering items that were not properly stored." On cue, Mrs. Haverford huffs, placing her hands on her hips. "Based on what we saw, only a handful of items could be saved, and we fully intend to restore them. No one wants to come in and remove years' worth of traditions and memories, but safety is also a concern." The room falls silent at the information. Thankfully Mayor Desmond comes to my rescue.

"Safety is and will always be this town's priority." He leans forward making eye contact with Mrs. Haverford. Turning back toward me, he says, "We appreciate your diligence and transparency with this council. All of this is cause for concern."

Nodding, I agree with him. "This is a minor setback, but I'm fully committed to this project," straightening up I try to project confidence. "Going forward, I think the best thing we can do is to create our very own custom pieces to be built to replace and revitalize the Christmas Spectacular." Several people are nodding their heads in agreement and a renewed sense of conviction that this *can* be done.

I will be the one to do it.

"And who do you have in mind to complete these custom projects?" Mr. Brown speaks up, asking the one question I'm worried about. Because I have a feeling they aren't going to like my answer.

"Well, due to such short notice, I'm afraid there aren't many options-" but before I can finish, Mrs. Haverford interrupts, yet again. She's really pushing my patience.

"Stop right there. My nephew can do it. He's a town native and also happens to be a carpenter. He just moved back into town and is trying to build his business. He'll do the job." Just looking at the set of her shoulders and the bob of her head while she spoke was all the information I needed to know that there would be no stopping this.

You've got to be kidding me.

The last thing I need is for Lori Haverford's nephew to be all in my business and report back to her about all the changes I'm making.

Old Mrs. Clinton leans forward, her face sweet with her wrinkled smile. "Oh, Levi is back in town? He's such a nice young man. We've missed him since he left for that city." Pointing her finger and shaking it like only a grandma can, she says, "I knew he'd come back. They never stray far for long."

Mayor Desmond stands clapping his hands in finality. "It's settled then. Levi will build these custom pieces for the Spectacular." He turns toward Lori. "Are you certain Levi can do this?"

She nods vehemently. "I'll make sure of it. You can count on Levi."

Somehow I get the feeling that everything is about to change.

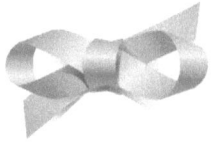

Chapter Two

Levi

"Watch out, coming through!" The box I'm carrying from the moving truck is so large I can't see over the top. "Wide load," I bellow while attempting to contort my body with the box at just the right angle to make it through the doorway.

"Okay Levi, just go straight. No, straight. What the hell, man?" Greyson's voice is obviously irritated at my lack of maneuvering. It's not like he gave the best directions since I walked straight into the wall, bouncing back while somehow managing to not drop the box.

"I'm good. Absolutely nothing to worry about," I chuckle as Greyson grabs my shoulders and moves me a step over.

Lightly pushing my back, he says, "Now go straight, dumbass." I'd laugh if the box wasn't so damn heavy. What the hell did I pack in here anyway?

Setting the box in the bedroom at the back of the unit, I take a look around at my new home. The duplex is small but was recently updated. Updated for Rose Prairie at least. The oven is at minimum ten years old, the floors are a mixture of carpet and linoleum, and the walls have been painted a bright white. It's not much, but it'll do. There aren't many options in Rose Prairie, so finding this place was a miracle.

Rose Prairie wasn't bad to grow up in, just quiet. After a while, that silence can become deafening. Also being in your twenties and living in a small town with the only girls you know being the ones that you watched pick their nose in first grade kind of puts a damper on all things dating. Two years after getting out of this small town, here I am. Right back where I started.

Greyson comes stomping in with the last of the boxes, placing them in the corner. "This is it," he says while removing his ball cap and pushing his hair back. "Why'd you have to move back again? Not that I'm not happy you're back," he clarifies. "I figured you'd want to stay away for good."

Greyson is my best friend and has been since diapers. He did his own time away from Rose Prairie when he went to our town's rival college forty-five minutes away. That must have been far enough away for him since he found himself right back where he started after graduating. He's been helping me unload boxes most of the evening, the winter sun having retreated hours ago. I've been told someone lives next door, but no one's come out to greet me—which is odd in a town like this one.

"City wasn't for me, remember? The people weren't as friendly, not to mention there were just too damn many of them." Coupled with the fact that the small custom furniture business I was hired to went under due to poor management. I could've found another job, but the pull back to this place couldn't be ignored. Swatting at his arm, I add, "Plus, I guess I missed seeing your ugly mug every day." Greyson just chuckles, walking out of the room back towards the front of the unit. I follow after him, making our way out the front door.

Seeing Greyson off with a wave, I close the door to the moving truck as my phone rings. Fishing it from my pocket, the screen lights up with Aunt Lori's face plastered across the screen. My mom's sister is a busybody, but we love her. Answering the call, I hold the phone to my ear. "Hey, Aunt Lo. What's up?"

"Oh, thank goodness you answered," she croons. "I have the best news." Her high pitched voice is telling me that she's excited about whatever she's about to share with me.

"Oh really?" Stepping through the front door, I close it behind me before plopping down on the giant brown monstrosity that is my couch.

"Yes," she squeals. "I just got you a job working on a project for the Christmas Spectacular! Isn't that just wonderful?"

Knowing my aunt, there's no way I'm going to talk my way out of this one. Especially when she says it's for the Christmas Spectacular. I don't think I know anyone more passionate about our town's traditions than her. That woman would do whatever it took to keep everything just as it is. Sighing, I respond. "And what is this job, exactly?"

"I'm so glad you asked," her words are fast and clipped. "The city has hired a new girl to be the event coordinator. And Miss Williams," she hisses, "has decided to throw everything out! Can you believe that? Anyway, she wants to create custom pieces to replace the classics we all know and love." She clicks her tongue, chastising whoever this Miss Williams person is. "That's where you come in. I volunteered you to be the carpenter involved in the project. It's only fitting to have a founding member's descendent be the one to make it. And you being back in town and all. It's kismet," she gushes.

Shaking my head, I know there's nothing I can do. She's completely blocked any arguments I could've potentially made. I've been cornered. Apparently, I take too long to respond because she's quickly asking if I'm still there.

I've got no choice.

"Yeah, I'm here. When do I start?" Christmas Eve is three weeks away, so it would have to be soon. I'd wanted to spend some time reacquainting myself with small-town life, but it looks like I won't have time for that now.

"Wonderful," she cheers. "I told the board you would be available starting as soon as possible. You've already gotten settled right?" she asks. Looking around at the furniture and boxes stacked in every direction, I would say otherwise.

"Just got the truck unloaded," I admit.

"Perfect timing then! I told Miss Williams that you would meet her at the warehouse tomorrow morning. You know the one? That large, green metal building off Main Street. Back towards Pinehurst?"

"Yeah, I know it." My free hand is squeezing the bridge of my nose, eyes squinting.

"Don't be late. And be sure to keep an eye out for that girl. I don't trust her."

Putting on my best-placating tone, I respond. "Yes ma'am."

Well, looks like my December is about to be all booked up.

. . ⚬⚬ . .

BRIGHT AND EARLY THE next morning—against my will—I arrive at the warehouse, coffee in hand. Knowing my aunt, she most likely appointed me as the man for the job without consulting anyone else, so I stopped by the coffee and book shop Tall, Dark, and Coffee and picked up some mochas—because everyone loves a mocha right? If I'm going to be working with Miss Williams for the next three weeks, I might as well try to make a good impression.

She's not here yet, so let the waiting game commence. It's not long before a white sedan pulls in next to my beat up truck. Something about it looks familiar, but nothing springs to mind. I'm sure it'll hit me the minute I stop trying to place it.

Huffing a breath, I grab the hot drinks and step out of the truck. *Here we go.*

Hearing a door click, I walk around the parked car just as Miss Williams climbs out. *Whoa. She's a stunner.* The woman scowling at me is quite possibly one of the most beautiful women I have ever seen in my life. And the way her eyes rake up and down my body with a hint of animosity has me grinning like a fool.

I love a challenge.

"Let me guess," she animatedly places her finger on her chin as she pretends to think, "you're Lori Haverford's nephew. The carpenter?"

Holy hell, I love a girl with spunk.

"The one and only," I reply bright and cheery—somehow knowing this will annoy her—and my smile widens. "Levi's the name. If you were wondering."

"I wasn't." Her quick response has me biting off a chuckle. She either really hates me or isn't a morning person. I guess she could be both. *And wouldn't I like to find out.* "I'm Samantha, but you can call me Sammie. I hope you know what you're doing because I'm not playing around here."

Clearly, she's all business. Dressed in blue jeans and work boots with a green tattered hoodie spotted with old oil stains on the front, she looks like a hands-on type of person.

I like a girl who is willing to get a little dirty.

Focus Levi.

"Yeah, I know what I'm doing, don't worry." Holding out the coffee towards her, I say, "Coffee? I stopped to pick up some before I got here. Figured I'd give a peace offering for coming into your project uninvited."

Those blue eyes squint at me, her face pinched. God, she's so pretty. Blue eyes and dark hair are my kryptonite and she's got the biggest eyes I've ever seen. Her hair is a dark brown; it almost looks black andt falls to her shoulder blades. And her skin? God, wouldn't I love to caress every inch of it. She has the complexion of a person who spends time in the sun making those eyes stand out even more. She's got the perfect amount of curves, from what I can see from her hoodie and jeans that is. It's not going to be a hardship to wake up and see her every day.

After a few seconds, her hand reaches out to grab the cup I'm holding out to her. Our fingers brush, setting off sparks."Thanks." Her voice has softened, and I wonder if she felt the same thing I did. I'm close enough to see hints of freckles across the bridge of her nose, and there's one on her neck that I'm dying to get my mouth on. "Let's stop standing around and get to work." She turns, closing her car door, before leading me up to the warehouse and stepping inside.

Musty air slams into my face as I enter the giant building, making me cough. "Holy hell, did something die in here?" I ask.

Sammie chuckles as she flips on the light. "So it seems," she sighs. "They've lived a long, hard life, but their time has come. We're thinking of hosting a funeral." *She's funny too.* "But this is also why you're here. All of this has been left in here to disintegrate all year, every year for who knows how long. Most of it can't be saved, so we're going to have to rebuild it ten times better from the ground up." She leads me down the aisle where I can see all the damage she's talking about. It's really sad seeing these decorations in such a state. No wonder they need me.

"I can see that." Leaning close I examine Frosty, the once-jolly snowman. Now, his smile is droopy and that's definitely mildew splattered across his face. "So what are you thinking? What's the goal?" Knowing what she's wanting to achieve will help with the designs and creativity.

She takes a sip of her coffee and I can tell the minute it hits her tongue. She tries to hide her surprise, but I catch that moment of recognition. *I think I just did something right.* Swallowing, she replies, "I'm looking to transform the town square into a Winter Wonderland, the likes of which no one has ever seen before. If that means working all day and night for the next three weeks, then that's what I'll do. If that's something you can't do, then I don't need you. I'll do it myself." She's full of determination, I'll give her that.

Smirking at her I have to remind myself to thank my aunt for being such a busybody and setting me up with this magnificent spitfire of a woman.

Chapter Three

Sammie

This day calls for fast food. Greasy, fattening, and delicious fast food. Rose Prairie doesn't have many options in terms of variety, so burgers and fries it is.

Spending all day with Levi was mentally, physically, and emotionally exhausting. Lori Haverford failed to mention that her nephew happened to be tall, built, and gorgeous. He also seems to be a genuinely nice person, which made it difficult to keep that wall up. A few times I found myself slipping and I had to force myself to remember that he was a spy. Obviously not a real spy, but his aunt is my enemy. Not in life—that's a bit dramatic—but in this project she's my nemesis.

He's just so good-looking. Honestly, I was expecting a middle-aged, receding hairline, burly type of man—someone similar to my uncle. Boy was I wrong. Levi is well over six feet tall, far from balding with no visible gut, and is in his twenties. He's got these chocolate brown eyes, a strong jaw peppered with stubble, and chestnut brown hair. I'm a red-blooded straight woman and having him so close by all day was distracting.

Turning into the parking lot of my apartment, the headlights flash across a familiar truck. And the familiar face sitting in the truck? Levi. Confusion floods my body. Why is Levi in my driveway?

Pulling up next to him, Levi breaks out into laughter. A head thrown back, body shaking type of laugh. What could he possibly find so funny? Snatching the bags out of the front seat and grabbing my drink, I walk directly to the man laughing hysterically in the cab of his truck. Food bag in hand, I knock on his window. Levi lowers it, laughing the entire time. "What are you doing at my apartment?" I ask angrily.

This throws Levi into another fit of laughter, his deep baritone voice ringing out. "Oh, this is too good." He actually slaps his knee. Sure, this is a real knee-slapper— my face says otherwise.

"No, seriously. What are you doing here?"

Levi takes a deep breath, placing a large hand on his chest as his cackling dies down. "Whew, your face was hilarious. Did you know your eyebrows get all crinkly and your nose scrunches up when you get confused?" I scowl at him as he cracks himself up again recalling my exact facial expression at seeing him here.

Fighting the urge to put my hand on my hip, I snap, "Will you just answer my question?"

"Alright, alright," he concedes, hands raised in surrender. Coughing away the rest of his chuckle he says the last thing I expected. "I live here."

Rose Prairie is a small town, but I couldn't imagine it being *this* small. What are the odds that the man I don't want to work with, appointed by a lady who hates me, just happens to move in right next door? We literally share a wall.

Shocked, I'm in utter disbelief. "Here? You live here?" My voice sounds panicky and that's because I'm panicking. First, I will be spending the next three weeks working closely with this man. Second, he looks like he just stepped out of a photoshoot for Hot Men Who Work With Their Hands Illustrated, which actually sounds like a good name for a magazine. And third, he lives right next door. I'll never be able to get away from him and that could be a bad thing. A very bad thing.

Yeah, for my lady bits. Not helpful Sammie.

Those deep brown eyes of his glide over my face, no doubt taking in the crazy lady standing outside his window. "Yep," he says, his lips popping on the p. "Moved in last night."

How in the world had I not known that he moved in? Thinking back to last night, I realize that I was at the City Council reporting on the state of the decorations. Sure, I saw the moving truck when I pulled up, but the lights were off and everything was quiet, so I figured whoever it was just dropped their stuff off. Never would I have imagined that Levi was my new neighbor.

Dumbfounded, all I can do is stare at him with my mouth opening and closing like a fish. Needing to say something, anything to get me out of here, I huff, "Well, you better keep the noise down. I won't hesitate to complain to Jim." Jim is the landlord. I've lived here for a year now and as landlords go, Jim's a good one. He checks in regularly to make sure everything in the unit is running fine and that I'm not having any problems, plus the rent is reasonable.

"Oh, I don't doubt it." He rolls his window up in my face, removing his keys from the ignition and opening the door. Stepping back, Levi gets out of his truck and stands there looking down at me. This is when I realize that I didn't step back far enough and my face is literally in his chest. How does he smell this good after walking around a musty warehouse all day?

Get a hold of yourself.

Blinking rapidly to knock some sense into myself, I turn and stride to my apartment door without another word. Unable to stop myself, I glance over my shoulder at him. Levi is still standing where I left him, arms crossed as he watches me walk away with a hint of a smirk on his face.

· · ∽ · ·

QUINN IS WAITING FOR me the next morning outside the local coffee shop I worked at before landing my dream job. Today, we are walking the town square to take measurements for the layout and to give us an idea of how large to make our new decorations. Since my apartment is only several blocks away, I thought it'd be a good idea to walk through the town.

That was a mistake.

Recent December drizzles left the sidewalks a muddy mess, completely coating my sneakers. The black leggings I'm wearing aren't thick enough for the cutting wind, but luckily my trusty puffy coat did its job and kept me warm and toasty.

Greeting Quinn with a quick hug, we step into the best coffee spot in town: Tall, Dark, and Coffee. A chain coffee shop has recently moved into town, but their drinks are too sweet and the atmosphere lacks a certain charm. Say what you want about Rosies, but they're loyal. The only people seen going into the new place are the ones that are driving through and don't know any better.

"How's the carpenter guy? Weren't you supposed to meet him yesterday?" Warm drinks in hand, Quinn and I sit at a small table in the corner of the shop beside the window. We have the perfect view of the town square and I can't stop myself from picturing it all lit up for Christmas.

My eyes roll so hard there's no way Quinn didn't notice. "Ugh, yes," I groan. She leans forward in anticipation. "He's going to make everything so much more difficult." Her gasps make me think that she's thinking about the project while I'm really thinking about my personal life.

"No! He's that bad huh?" She pushes up her sliding glasses taking a sip of her peppermint latte. "I just knew Mrs. Haverford was going to try to drag you down."

"He's not bad in the way you think. Levi's actually really nice. Almost too nice. He brought me coffee as some kind of white flag to apologize for his aunt."

"Then what kind of bad is he?" Her eyebrow raises with her question giving me a "do tell" kind of look.

"It's just that..." I pause, trying to come up with the right words. "He's just... I think..."

Impatient, Quinn butts in. "Oh, cut the shi- crap. Tell me!" One thing I appreciate about Quinn is her unwillingness to put up with bullshit. She won't let me sidestep an issue; she'll confront me about it.

"He's hot!" *Too loud.* I said that too loud and now everyone in the shop pauses to look at me. *Someone shoot me now.* Leaning in, I whisper, "He's like, really good-looking. Almost to the point of distraction. Believe me when I say that it was hard to not stare at him as we walked through the warehouse."

"Ooh, we love a hot man. So, how is this a problem? I'm not seeing an issue here."

"Quinn, I have to hate him. He's the enemy. He's her *nephew!* I just know she's going to want any details about my plans and that's her way to do it."

Quinn raises a skeptical brow at me. "I think you're reading way too much into this."

"I don't think I am." Jutting my chin in defiance I stare across the table at my assistant. "This is my dream job and I'm not going to let anyone ruin it for me. Even if he's the ridiculously hot nephew of Lori Haverford."

After finishing our drinks and waving goodbye to Cara—my former boss and the owner of the coffee shop—we cross the street to the square. This place is one of the main reasons I chose Rose Prairie to be my new home. It reminds me of Stars Hollow from Gilmore Girls with its large trees and beautiful white gazebo in the middle. In the spring, magnificent flowers bloom in a vibrant patchwork of colors. In the summer, live music is played from its steps while people sit around on their blankets enjoying the summer breeze. It's just so damn picturesque.

Breaking out the measuring tape, we get to work. Quinn holds one end while I hold the other, calling out the numbers for Quinn to jot down in her notebook. It's vital that I get everything just right.

"Think we got it all?" Quinn saunters over to me as I scan the area.

"Maybe." We both stand there looking around when I realize that we missed a spot stretching across the middle of the square. "Oh, we forgot to do this one." Pointing to the area I'm referring to, she nods her head and reaches out for the start of the measuring tape while I walk it across the grass, the yellow ruler trailing after me. Unfortunately, I have to maneuver around a large tree.

I've never been the most graceful human being, so I carefully watch my step as I pass through the maze of roots jutting up from the ground. I must've not been careful enough because before I know what's happening, my ass lands right in a giant, slippery puddle of mud.

I hear Quinn laugh, covering her mouth as she jogs over to me. There's no way I'll be able to get myself out of this unscathed. The ground surrounding me is completely soaked, not a dry spot to place my hand to try to heave myself up. But before Quinn can come to my rescue, the squish of mud under shoes comes up from behind me.

Turning, I look up and see Levi standing over me. Of course, it's him. Who else could it be? Surely not any of the other five thousand people who live here.

"Are you okay? I saw you go down from across the street."

Just wonderful. "Fine," I say through gritted teeth.

"Oh my god, Sammie! Are you alright?" Quinn comes running over to me and I can see the instant she notices Levi. Her finger pushes up the bridge of her glasses as her eyes travel up and down his body. "Hi, I'm Quinn," she introduces herself, holding her hand out to Levi.

"Not the time, Quinn," I mutter. A little louder I say, "Can I get some help here?"

Strong hands slide under my arms as Levi lifts me out of the puddle and helps me to solid ground.

My entire backside is completely caked in mud. Not only am I wet and cold, but also mortified. *Why oh why did Levi have to see that?*

Gathering my pride, I turn and look directly into his beautiful face. I've tried avoiding looking directly at him, worried that I won't be able to look away. His brown hair is longer on top and shorter on the sides, styled but a bit messy. His strong jaw is accentuated with light scruff. And those eyes? Whoever said brown eyes aren't pretty haven't seen his yet. I could swim in those eyes, all swirling shades of amber and a deep rich brown that makes me think of chocolate.

Momentarily stunned, I spend too long admiring him. Thankfully, Quinn elbows me in the side, effectively breaking my focus on his face. Quickly looking away, I clear my throat. "Um, thank you for your help."

"No problem." His smile is kind and warm as we look at one another.

"You should probably get cleaned up," Quinn cuts in. How long have Levi and I been staring at each other?

What in the world is going on with me? Get a hold of yourself, Sammie.

Levi glances around at the parking spots lining the street. "How'd you get here? I thought I saw your car in the driveway before I left."

"That's because you did," I sigh. "I walked here this morning." Turning toward my assistant, I ask, "Can you take me home Quinn?"

"Can't," she replies. "I rode my bike from campus." *Just Perfect.*

"Come on then." Levi turns around, hand waving over his shoulder as he calls, "I'm parked right over here."

Opening my mouth about to protest, he stops and turns. "There's no way I'm letting you walk home. Come on, get in the truck."

Huffing a breath, I weigh my options. I could walk home, literally freezing my ass off or I could take a short ride in Levi's truck.

"Sammie!" Levi calls as he stands in front of his truck. "Don't make me carry you." His tone is teasing, but his eyes say that he will actually pick me up and carry me to his truck.

Rolling my eyes, I stomp to his truck. Fine by me if he wants his seat all muddy.

Chapter Four

Levi

After working all week, Greyson and I sit at the bar of Bottom's Up drinking beers while a football game plays on the tv overhead. This week was spent spending every day with Sammie, going over the designs of the new decorations and the overall layout of the square for the Christmas Spectacular. She's a bit bossy but she has a clear vision. The town is going to be wowed by what she can do.

"Wait, so your aunt put you up to this?" This is the first time we've been able to meet up since he helped me move in. I've spent the last ten minutes filling him in on my first week back in town.

"You know my aunt. She doesn't take no for an answer." Swigging down some beer, I place my half-empty glass on the bar top. "But you won't see me complaining." Thinking of Sammie brings a grin to my face that Greyson catches.

Stopping mid-drink, Greyson points at me. "What was that for?" Setting his drink down, his voice lowers. "You have a thing for that chick?" he asks.

I shrug. "I can't help myself, man. Sammie is the most beautiful woman I've ever seen. Plus, she seems to hate my guts which makes her even more attractive." Thinking about how she huffed and puffed on the ride home with her ass covered in mud has me chuckling. There's just something about this woman that I can't get over.

"You're a sucker for punishment is what you are."

"Oh, and get this," I say. "She lives in the duplex next door. She was so mad when she found out too. It was damn cute."

Full of skepticism, he turns to me. "So let me get this straight: you're working with this woman, find her attractive even though she doesn't like you, and she lives next door?"

"She likes me. She just doesn't know it yet."

He shakes his head as he brings his beer to his mouth. "You're an idiot."

"I'm telling you, she's the girl I've been looking for." Deep in my gut I know it's true. Ever since she stepped out of that car and looked at me with that glare on her face, I was done for.

Greyson just sighs. "Tell me again in two weeks and I'll believe you." He's skeptical and he has a right to be. He thought he'd found the one for him, but that was before she left him for another man.

"Deal."

.. ❧ ..

THE LAST SEVERAL DAYS we've been working to get the new attractions put together. Today we're working on creating giant, glowing ornaments that will be grouped on either side of the sidewalk. Yesterday, we worked together on the frames. Sammie secured the wood pieces with screws and wood glue while I measured and made the cuts with the saw. She wasn't lying when she said she didn't need me— she knows exactly what she's doing.

We're dividing and conquering. Right now, she's painting the pegboard that the lights will be strung through, and I can't help watching her as she does. I'm supposed to be framing the gingerbread houses that will be large enough for people to walk through, but I'm finding myself distracted as she moves. Her hair is pulled back into a ponytail and she's wearing a puffy vest to keep the sleeves of her coat from getting paint on them. Her jeans are hugging the curve of her ass, splotches of old paint covering them. She's stunning.

Some men prefer their women all dolled up, but I've always found myself drawn to a more low-key, natural look. And boy does Sammie fit that mold. Sure, she dresses up now and then, especially when she's not doing manual labor, but she's even more appealing to me without all that. I want someone willing to work beside me and not watching from afar, too dainty to get her hands messy. This just solidifies that she's the girl I'm looking for.

"How are the houses coming along?" Sammie's back is to me as she hollers at me. She's keeping a strict schedule and the goal today is to finish the ornaments and the gingerbread houses. Quinn has enlisted the help of the art department at the Rosewood College and they are coming to decorate the houses to look exactly like homemade gingerbread houses. They've been working on creating smaller pieces that will be attached: gumdrops, mints, candy canes, and whatever else goes on a gingerbread house. From what I understand, the only thing they'll need is a drill.

"Almost done getting the walls ready." To emphasize my point, I drive the screws into the wood, the noise of the drill downing out all sound.

"Better hurry. This *needs* to be done today." She looks over her shoulder at me, and I can't help but smile at her. She rolls her eyes as expected, but I think I'm starting to wear her down. She's not as grumpy as she was last week.

At least I think she isn't.

"Yes, ma'am." She tries to hide it, but I can see a hint of a smile cross that beautiful mouth of hers.

Thirty minutes later, she's gotten the ornaments painted and has moved on to priming the plywood walls for the houses. She told the college that everything would be ready for them and all they would need to do is place the decorations and that meant getting everything painted the distinctive shade of brown.

In no time at all the wall frames are finally ready to be put together. "Sammie, I'm gonna need your help with this." She finishes spraying the last board and stands walking over toward me.

Clapping her hands together she says, "Where do you need me?" Immediately my mind goes to her laying on my bed, naked and ready for me.

Fuck. Get your head out of the gutter.

My face is suddenly hot and I clear my throat. "Um, I need you to help me stand this wall up here," I point to the one at her feet, "and hold it in place while I lift this side and secure them." On the count of three, we lift the wall into a standing position. "You okay for me to do the other one?" I ask.

"Sure. I've got this." Her head nods as if reassuring herself. I don't want her to get hurt, so I work as quickly as I can to lift the other frame into place.

"Let me know if it gets too heavy."

Sammie grimaces as we fit the frames together. "I said I've got it," she snaps.

Oh this woman is stubborn.

We work together, quickly getting the three structures standing. Her design has the houses in varying sizes to make them enjoyable for people of all ages. The smallest one is big enough for toddlers to waddle through, and the cuteness of it all makes me grin. She really has thought of everything.

Glancing down at my watch, I realize it's lunchtime. "Is the paint dry yet?"

Sammie wanders over, examining the slabs of wood, gently touching different spots to check if the paint is dry. "Nah. They still need a bit more time."

Perfect.

"Well, why don't we go get some lunch?" I ask. I want to sit down and have a full conversation without having to talk over power tools. And selfishly I want her attention all to myself. Sammie turns and stares at me, contemplation written all over her face. I *need* this time with her. I'd be kicking myself if I never got the chance to get to know her. "C'mon," I jest. "It's my treat. Lunch never hurt anyone."

She purses her lips for a moment before finally answering. "Sure, we can have lunch." Pleasure zings through me and I have to fight the urge to fist-pump the air like John Bender at the end of The Breakfast Club.

This is my shot and I'm not going to blow it.

Chapter Five

Sammie

Honey's Diner is a quaint little spot just down Main Street. Honey, the owner, is a sweet lady who's a staple in this town. She's one of the first people I met in Rose Prairie, and she holds a special place in my heart.

It might be a mistake to come to lunch with Levi, but he's been so kind that I couldn't say no. Levi might be Lori Haverford's nephew, but he certainly isn't anything like her. He genuinely wants to see this be a success and is on board with my ideas, often adding to them and making them better. If he's reporting back to his aunt, at this point I don't care.

The diner is busy with the lunch rush, but we manage to grab a small, two-person booth. Honey's is kitschy, decorated with honeybees and honeycombs. Even the vinyl on the booths and chairs is a golden shade of honey. The waitresses wear 50's inspired dresses complete with lace socks and Mary Jane shoes. I absolutely love it.

"Have you been here before?" Levi settles into the booth across from me, reaching for a menu stacked behind the napkin dispenser.

"Yep." He hands me a menu and I glance at the lunch options. "It was the first place I stopped when I got to town. It's one of the things that made me pick Rose Prairie as my new home."

"Where are you from?" His question doesn't feel forced. He genuinely would like to know. *Why does this feel like a date?* Maybe I should have been clear about what this lunch is. Lunch, and nothing more.

Or so I'm telling myself.

Taking a deep breath, I try to decide how much to tell him. The wall I've tried to build between us is quickly crumbling the longer I spend time with him. He never seems fazed by my gruffness towards him, if anything it makes him like me even more. There's no way I'll be able to keep this up much longer. Resigned, I answer, "I'm originally from Chicago. I grew up there."

His eyes snap up to mine over his menu, a look of interest on his face. But before he can respond, a beautiful blond waitress stops in front of us.

"Levi? Oh my gosh, I heard you were back in town!" Feeling like an outsider, I watch as Levi stands and gives our waitress a quick hug.

"Hey, June. Yeah, I moved back last week. It's been pretty busy." Is it just me, or does Levi seem uncomfortable? His hands are resting on his hips and he's shifting his weight between his feet. His eyes meet mine for a split second and I suddenly don't feel so out of place. "June, this is Sammie. Sammie, this is June."

"Hi," I say as I manage an awkward wave. "Nice to meet you."

"Well, hi there." June is the classically beautiful girl next door. Even dressed in her work outfit, she's gorgeous. She's got a kind smile and dimples that make her cute as a button.

Levi slides back into the booth as June pulls out her notepad, readying to take our orders. "What would you guys like today?"

We both order glasses of water and I choose the soup and sandwich option while Levi goes for a heartier meal of chicken fried chicken.

After June heads back to the kitchen to put in our order, I look at Levi. "Is she an ex or something?" A pang of jealousy stabs my chest, but I have no right to be jealous of anything. *This isn't even a date*, I remind myself.

He chuckles, hand scraping his jaw. "It was a long time ago. We dated for a couple of months in High School." He shakes his head. "Anyway, you're from Chicago? What brought you to Rose Prairie then?"

Hmm. Do I go into detail or not? I might as well blow through the last semblance of the wall I've made like the Kool-Aid man. *Screw it.*

"I left the city because it wasn't for me. All my life I grew up wishing to be somewhere different from where I was. Chicago was just too large and stifling. Small towns hold more appeal for me, so I left." I shrug.

A crooked smile pulls at his mouth as he looks at me, his eyes conveying a softness. *God, I could melt in that gaze.* "What about you? Why'd you move back here?"

Levi leans back into the booth cushion behind him. "Well," he sighs, "it's very similar to your reason actually. It was too quiet growing up and I longed for something more. But that something more ended up being too much and I couldn't resist the pull back to this place."

Color me shocked. Levi and I have something in common.

"So, what's the deal with the Christmas Spectacular?" he asks, changing the subject.

"What do you mean?"

He leans forward, elbows crossed on the table. "You're just so passionate about it. I don't think I've seen anyone want something more than you want this." How is he able to see me so clearly when I've been nothing but a—let's be honest—bitch to him?

"Whoa, that's a serious question," I tease. "Do you want the real answer or the boring one?"

"Real, obviously. How else am I going to get to know you?" His grin lights up his face as he winks at me. An honest-to-god wink.

I think I'm going to combust now.

I can't help but chuckle. "The real reason is that I love Christmas. I love everything about it. There's just something about it that transforms everything for me. The beauty that the joy of Christmas brings to people, the glow of the lights during the dark of night, the quiet stillness of snowfall..." I sigh, "it's everything."

Tilting his head, Levi examines me, those brown eyes so intense it's like he's seeing right through me. "You know what, Sammie? I think you're one of the most interesting people I've ever met."

Whoa, where did that come from?

Luckily, I'm saved by June when she returned with our food. We dive into our meal, both hungry from the hard work we'd done today. The potato soup is creamy and delicious and works to warm me up.

"I have to ask," he says after cutting a slice of chicken, "how do you know so much about construction?"

"That's an easy one. I learned from my uncle. He owns a little shop that my cousins and I grew up running around in. To keep us out of trouble, he'd have us work on things around the store to keep us busy." I scoop up another mouthful of soup. "What about you?"

He finishes chewing his bite before he answers. "I took a shop class in high school and was good at it. Working with my hands came naturally to me, so I kept up with it. Spent a couple of years in the program at Rosewood. Then, I worked for a bit in town after I graduated, but I took a job in the city for a couple of years."

"What'd you do there?" I'm finding myself genuinely curious about the man sitting across from me.

"I worked at a custom furniture place. The owner ran it into the ground, which was a bummer, but I was already wanting to come home at that point. That became the excuse I needed to come back here." His eyes meet mine; his voice is soft as he says, "I'm glad I did though. I wouldn't have come across such a beautiful spitfire to keep me on my toes."

Beautiful? Spitfire? Is this what he thinks of me?

My throat is suddenly dry, and I quickly chug the rest of my water, the ice splashing into my face, causing me to choke. Water spews up my nose and there's no stopping the harsh coughs that leave my body. Water drenches the front of my shirt as I work to get myself under control.

Levi reaches across the table, placing his hand on my shoulder. "Are you okay?" His voice is gentle and kind as I continue hacking up my lungs. My face flushes red with embarrassment and lack of oxygen, and all I can do is nod while my body seems to expel some kind of demon.

"Goodness, do you guys need some more napkins?" June stops by our table as I continue to cough.

"Yes, please. And some more water." Levi answers, his hand never leaving my shoulder.

All I can think about is that hand, how warm it is, and the kindness of the man it belongs to. His thumb strokes back and forth along my collar bone and all my awareness shifts to that small caress.

What other kind of caress can he make? And why do I want it?

Finally regaining control, my cough slows just as June returns with the napkins and water. Levi's hand moves from my shoulder as he grabs a napkin and begins to clean up the wet table. Without his hand on me, I feel deprived of that connection. And I want it.

So much more than I should.

Chapter Six

Levi

After my lunch with Sammie, I couldn't get her out of my head.

She puts on this tough exterior, but she's started to open up. The way she would pause, her head tilting while she looked at me, made me think she was wondering how much to share with me. Like she was fighting with herself. She keeps her card close to her chest, but I'm willing to play her game. I'll wait her out, show her I'm the real deal and get her to open up even more to me.

There had been a moment when I'd wondered if I said too much, been too forward. But then she started choking on her water and all I could think about was comforting her until she calmed down. Something had flashed in her eyes, so quickly that I barely noticed, when my hand was on her shoulder.

A look that I wanted to see again.

The rest of the afternoon we worked on the houses. We'd managed to get them all built and ready for the Rosewood College art department to come up and attach their decorations. It'd been a long afternoon, both of us weary and tired at the end of the day.

Later that night, I check my pockets for my keys, and I get ready for dinner with my family. It's a weekly tradition for all of us to get together for a meal and now that I'm back in town

I'm expected to join. Honestly, I'm not looking forward to it. My aunt will be there, and I know she's going to hound me with questions on what's happening with the Christmas Spectacular and "that Miss Williams."

Heading to my beat-up Ford, I notice that Sammie isn't home. Absent-mindedly, I wonder where she is and what she's doing. I'm sure she's working on some of the smaller projects for the Spectacular. She's one focused woman and I find that attractive. Who am I kidding? I find everything about her attractive.

Sprinkles of snow are descending from the sky creating a light dusting that coats the grass. *Sammie would love this.* And there I go again thinking of her. *Dammit man, get a hold of yourself.*

My parents live in a white, two-story house with a wraparound porch. Their Christmas tree is lit in front of the bay windows looking out into the front yard. Garland hangs over the front door with poinsettias delicately placed and I can't help but think Sammie and my mom would get along great. Sammie and my aunt, however...

"I'm here," I call out while stomping snow from my boots before removing them and placing them under the bench next to the door.

Right on cue, the sound of nails scraping against the hardwood floors echoes through the house as the family dog, Lucky, runs as fast as his little legs can carry him. Lucky is a beagle that my parents picked up around five years ago off the side of a country road. He was cold and skinny and covered in fleas and ticks. It was a no-brainer to bring him home, and he's been a welcomed addition ever since.

"Hey, bud." Bending down I rub his ears as he tries to jump and lick all over me. He's at least seven years old now and should be slowing down, but he's still as spry as the day he came home.

After greeting Lucky, I head into the kitchen where my mom and aunt are hard at work. "Hi, Mom." Giving her a quick peck on the cheek before moving to hug my aunt. Donna Ross is one classy lady. She's the type of mom who looked fantastic wherever she went, even if it was running errands around town, she was always dressed to perfection.

"Hey, Aunt Lo." My aunt wraps me in a quick hug. My mother and her sister are very similar in looks, but my aunt is far more uptight than my mom. My sister and I didn't particularly like going over to Aunt Lo and Uncle Rob's house when we were younger because we would get in trouble for moving something a centimeter to the side. We love her, she's just...particular.

She pulls back, giving me an inquisitive eye. "Before you leave, I need to have a chat with you." Yeah, I saw this coming from a mile away.

"Sure thing."

I duck out of the kitchen as fast as I can before she ropes me into a conversation right then and there. Walking into the living room, my dad and sister are sprawled out on the couches watching a football game.

Paige is a few years younger than I am and is the apple of my dad's eye. She's a sport-playing, takes no shit type of woman. Which made for a lot of bruises growing up. She's always down for a beer, going for a run, or watching any type of sports team. Seriously, she'll sit and watch bowling if nothing else is on. And she gets *invested*. Yelling at the screen and chatting with the commentators, invested. She's in her last year at Rosewood College and is majoring in Sports Medicine to become a trainer, which suits her personality to a t.

Paige kindly lifts her legs for me to sit on the end of the couch—the nicest gesture I'm sure she'll make all day. "Hey, bro." She lives on campus, but she can often be found parked right here on the couch next to dad. "Oh, come on ref! That's a clear holding!" Paige sits up and angrily points at the tv screen where the play is under review.

Dad, as per usual, is a more laid back sports watcher. Always watching, but never commenting. It's funny to watch my dad and my sister watch a game together. Paige is dramatic and loud while dad is stoic and silent. I guess that's why they get along so well.

"Hey, son." I tend to take after my dad. Carter Ross is the chill, calm Dad. He's got dark hair and eyes while my mom and sister have light hair and eyes. Growing up, he had a full beard that he would carefully groom. As time passed, his beard got shorter and shorter. Maybe the speckles of gray hair are what eventually made him shave it all off.

One thing about coming to my parent's house for our weekly dinners is that they are loud. The ladies chat in the kitchen while preparing the food—well my mom and aunt, not Paige—the tv will be on any sports channel, and there will be yelling. Angry screams at the television, not with each other thankfully.

Dinner is special tonight since it's my first one since moving back into town. Mom made my favorite: pot roast. We all sit around the table, catching up with Dad's job as an accountant for several local businesses and Aunt Lo goes on and on about how the town is getting out of control since Mayor Desmond was elected.

After helping clean up after dinner, I hurriedly make my rounds of goodbyes. Just when I think I'm about to slip out without being harassed about the Christmas Spectacular, my aunt follows me out the front door with her coat wrapped tightly around her waist. "Now, Levi, just wait a minute." My back's to her, so I use the opportunity to silently curse before turning around.

"Yes, ma'am?" *Maybe if I play dumb, she'll get sidetracked...*

"I wanted to speak with you about the Christmas Spectacular. Didn't you remember?"

Feigning ignorance, I say, "Oh, yeah. That's right. I forgot."

"It's a good thing I caught you then!" She playfully smacks my arm, her grin wide. "Now, tell me. How's everything going?"

In the dark lighting of the driveway with the Christmas lights shining, my aunt looks so similar to my mom. She's really a lovely lady, even though she's meddlesome. She hasn't always been this way. After Uncle Rob died of a heart attack several years ago, she's taken to keeping busy: joining the city council and bustling around town getting into people's business.

"We're busy working," I point out. "Sammie's got some great ideas and we're seeing it through. I think it'll be great."

Pursed lips and eyes narrowing, my aunt stares at me. "You wouldn't be lying to your aunt now, would you? You know how much this Christmas Spectacular means to me."

Sighing, I rake my hand through my stubble. "No, Aunt Lori, I'm not lying. I think she's great. You should give her a chance. She's ambitious and creative..." I have to trail off because other attributes that don't need to be shared with my aunt keep popping up. *Sexy. Charming. Mysterious. Passionate.* "She'll be good for this town."

She clicks her tongue before turning and walking back up the drive and up the front steps. She turns around at the top of the stairs, "I guess we'll have to see if you're right."

· · ↬ · ·

INSTEAD OF HEADING straight home to an apartment full of unpacked boxes, I take a detour through town. Sometimes a nice drive around town in the dark is just the sort of thing you need to reset. Houses on either side of the street glisten with Christmas lights, invoking some of that beauty that Sammie spoke so passionately about.

Nearing the far side of town, I head in the direction of the Miller's house. Each year they set their yard up with decorations set to Christmas music, creating a show of lights. They've been setting it up for the past ten years since seeing it on the news and they couldn't get enough of it. There are several cars lined up on the curb watching the lights flash to the beat of the music.

Mr. Miller went all out this year. The whole front of the house is covered in lights with alternating rows of color. A giant Frosty is on the roof waving at passersby and there's even a little workshop with motorized elves working on toys. A miniature train is set up on the front lawn with Santa and his reindeer riding and waving as they pass by.

I don't stay long knowing there's a line already gathering behind me. On a whim, I decide to drive by the town square and look at the gingerbread houses in all their glory. The houses are completely decorated with swirly red mints, gumdrops, and sprinkles. They even added snow and ice detailing on the roof and eaves. They look great.

Just as I'm about to turn and head home, a movement and flash of light catches my eye. One of the large ornaments that Sammie was working on earlier are lit. My brows furrow in confusion because we haven't had time to put those lights up. Another quick movement catches my eye.

Is the ornament... *moving?*

Chapter Seven

Sammie

After completing the houses and ornaments, my evening was spent wandering down aisle after aisle at stores in Lake Elkins. It's about a thirty minute drive west, but it has more options for shopping than Rose Prairie. I was able to get many items from local stores, but today I'm picking up ones I can't find in town.

Trunk full of items, I make the drive back into town, the sun setting in my rear-view mirror. It doesn't take long before the Christmas Spectacular comes to mind. There's just so much left to be done and not enough time to do it. Levi and I have managed to get many of the items replaced and ready to go this week, but with one week left we're down to crunch time.

All I can think about on the drive is how we're not going to finish. That I'm not going to be able to fulfill my vision for the town square. All the extra time to think has created a rolling ball of anxiety in my gut.

We don't have enough time.

Tears sting my eyes as Christmas music plays through the speakers. *Toughen up, Sammie. You can do this, you can do this, you can do this...*

Instead of heading home as I should, I drive right to the town square hellbent on getting *something* accomplished tonight. Stopping in front of the gingerbread houses, I can't help but smile. They look absolutely amazing. Quinn did a great job in getting the college involved in this project and I think it's a nice touch.

Wandering through what we've already gotten done, we aren't as behind as I thought. Lamp posts are decorated with lit garlands wrapped around the tall poles. The snowflakes we managed to save from the warehouse have been revitalized and are sparkling in the moonlight as they hang from tree branches. Lights are strung along the sidewalks with candy cane hooks and the evergreen tree next to the gazebo is picturesque with the lights and ornaments hanging. The light dusting of snow this evening has everything looking just as magical as I envisioned.

Turning in a circle I try to pinpoint different things that need to be completed this week before the big reveal. The gazebo still needs to be decorated, Christmas lights still need to be strung overhead, and the light displays we ordered are waiting to be unpacked and set up. All of these are things that I can't do by myself. Scanning the area, my eyes rake over the large ornaments that Levi and I worked on. The peg boards were painted and placed over the frames we built together, all they need are the lights.

Which are in my trunk...

This is perfect. Stringing the lights through that pegboard will take some time and if I can get it done tonight, that'd be one less thing to worry about. Decision made, I march to my car to grab the lights. Plopping my purse in the backseat, I grab the bags with the things I need and get to work.

In designing the ornaments, Levi left a small hole in the bottom of each one that would help keep them level and also doubles as an easy way for the lights to be strung up and replaced when needed. They are already tilted on their sides and are just waiting for the lights.

Before crawling inside, I unroll a string of red lights and plug them into the outlet built in nearby. Each ornament will be a different color. Eventually, my goal is to have designs on each one, but this year due to time constraints, they'll have to be plain. Still beautiful, but plain.

It takes longer than I thought it would to get the lights through the holes. The bulbs fit just right, each one being snug enough that they won't fall out. After about thirty minutes, I have all one side completed.

How am I going to do the other side?

In order to complete the other half of the ornament, I need to get the side that's on the ground up so that I can string the lights. In a moment of sheer stupidity, I push the ornament upright, leaving the hole I climbed in through flush with the ground.

Clarity hits a split second too late and now I'm stuck inside a fucking ornament. Pushing against the side to tilt it back, the damn thing doesn't move. It's too heavy for me to push over on my own. Frantic, my hands fly to the pocket of my jeans in search of my phone. It's not there. My pockets are empty. Where the *hell* is my phone? Utter panic sets in when I remember my phone is safely tucked into my purse. Which is currently in the backseat of my car.

What the hell did I just do?

Shit, shit, shit.

The town square was dead when I got here. What are the odds that someone could be walking by? Hoping and praying that someone decided to go for a nice stroll through the winter night, I yell. "Hello? Is anyone there? Help!" Pushing against the side of the ornament with all my might it doesn't budge.

I'm well and truly stuck.

I yell for several more minutes to no avail. Not wanting to go hoarse, I decide to wait until I can hear voices before I start yelling again. With nothing better to do at the moment, I continue to push the bulbs through the holes until the entire thing is covered in lights.

It's okay, I tell myself. At least it's warm in here. And I know people will be showing up eventually, I just have to keep myself calm and not freak out. Which is easier said than done.

Deep breath in, deep breath out. Nice and calm. Deep breath in...

Nope, I can't do it. I told myself I wouldn't scream until I heard someone, but after what feels like forever stuck inside a glowing orb, I break. Pushing against the sides I scream for anyone to help me.

In an out-of-body experience, I picture a stranger stumbling on this giant glowing ball, shaking and moving with the voice of a crazy lady calling out for help. Struck by the visual and my panic, uncontrollable laughter takes over at the insanity of this situation. I laugh so hard that tears stream down my face and my abs start to hurt.

I'm laughing so much that I don't hear the scuffle of boots coming toward me.

A deep voice startles me, making me jump. "Hello? Is someone in there?" Oh, thank God. I'm being rescued.

"Yes!" I scream. "I'm in here!" Still chuckling, I push against the side making the ornament shake.

The steps are closer now. "Sammie? Is that you in there?"

Recognition floods through me. "Levi?" My face scrunches with embarrassment. Of course, it would be Levi to rescue me. It seems that he's the only person capable of coming to my rescue when I find myself in a predicament.

"Sammie, what the hell are you doing?" I can't tell if he's mad, frustrated, or titillated.

"Working on my tan, obviously." What's with all the questions? "Can you get me out or not?"

Footsteps walk around my cage almost like he's weighing his options. Wait, he won't leave me in here, will he? No, he couldn't possibly.

Panic springs up again at the thought. "Levi? You're going to get me out right?" My voice comes out high pitched with a hint of alarm.

He scoffs. "Of course I am. How else am I going to win you over?"

Butterflies erupt in my chest. He wants to win me over? Little does he know that he's already started to wear me down. I'm not this mean person, but I can't let Lori Haverford beat me. I *need* to prove her wrong about me. He just happens to be the middleman.

Within minutes, Levi tilts the ornament enough for me to squeeze out. Finally, I'm free. Wiping off my now dirty jeans, Levi watches me.

"Okay, I have to know. What were you doing?" He chuckles at the look of contempt on my face.

"If you must know, I was trying to get things done tonight so I wouldn't have to do them later. My smart self had to have the brilliant idea of tilting it over so I could finish putting the lights in. Only I closed myself inside and I couldn't get out and my phone's in my car. Happy?"

A look of concern crosses his face. "No, actually." His voice is deep and soft as he looks me in the eye. "I don't want you working out here without me."

"It needs to be done and I had the time to do it. I don't think that means you need to be with me." I'm a grown-ass woman who doesn't need a babysitter. A ridiculously hot babysitter, but still.

His handsome face softens. "We'll do it together from now on. I don't want you getting hurt or trapped again. You hear me?" His calloused hand reaches up and gently caresses my cheek.

Holy shit. Levi is so freaking sexy, even more so when he looks at me like this. Full of concern and longing. Stunned by the sudden pulsing in my panties, I'm left speechless at this turn of events.

Swallowing hard, I nod. "Okay."

Chapter Eight

Levi

The snow doesn't let up for the next several days, meaning all the outdoor work has been put on hold. Sammie isn't thrilled and has spent her time rampaging around the warehouse.

The morning after I found her inside the ornament, we loaded up the remaining ornaments from the town square and took them inside the warehouse. Not wanting her to be trapped in one again, I made a small stand for them to sit on, making it easier for her to sit inside to string up the lights.

Christmas Eve is three days away and the stress is starting to weigh down on all of us. Quinn has worked her magic and several students from Rosewood have stopped by to help decorate the pile of presents that will be stacked in the sleigh I'm currently building. Sammie's vision has the sleigh as part of a photo opportunity for visitors. It will be pulled by the lit reindeer the girls set up yesterday and pictures will be taken by the photography students from Rose Prairie High. The proceeds will be donated to the local food pantry—which proves that she's hiding that warm heart of hers.

I just wish she'd show it to me.

The chatter of the warehouse quickly dies the moment the door slams shut, a very familiar outline standing there glancing around the room. Aunt Lori. Lord help me.

"My, oh my. Look at all this!" Her perky voice is the only sound in the room besides the clicking of her heels against the concrete floor. Only my mom and Aunt Lori would wear heels when snow is falling.

No one says anything. Not a sound comes from Sammie or Quinn or the half-dozen other people working on the presents. To make things less awkward, I put down my power tools and walk toward my aunt, giving her a quick hug. "Hey, Aunt Lori. What brings you here?" Maybe the quicker I get her talking, the quicker she'll leave. Sammie's back is ramrod straight, hands on hips as she eyes my aunt. Clearly, there's no love lost.

"Well, I just wanted to come by and take a look at everything. There's a city council meeting tonight and I wanted to get a first-hand look at how things are coming along." She glances around at the current works in progress, spinning in a complete circle.

Essentially, what she's seeing is chaos. Lights are laid out in long strips against the side wall, ready and waiting to be strung up from the flagpole in the square to create a giant Christmas tree made of lights. Discarded boxes are next to the door waiting to be transported to the recycling center, and Sammie and Quinn are covered in red paint from working on the wooden cutouts of Mr. and Mrs. Claus. The last-minute addition was easy enough to make and the oval cut-out for faces was straightforward.

"Mrs. Haverford. Thank you for stopping by." Sammie's voice is strained as she greets my aunt with a cautious grin. Thankfully, everyone starts getting back to work, their banter as they wrap presents easing the tension.

"Oh, there you are Miss Williams. I didn't notice you with all this...mess laying around. How nice to see you working so hard." Oh boy. This can't be going anywhere good. I'm surprised Sammie's face hasn't turned bright red and that steam isn't pouring out of her ears.

Sammie's smile tightens as she says, "Of course. We're nearing the end. Just getting the last touches ready for when the snow stops. Is there anything, in particular, I can help you with?"

"Goodness me, no." she chuckles. "Just curious. I noticed when I stopped in at Mama's Cakes that the square was looking a little..." she pauses, searching for the right word. "Bare."

"Nothing to worry about here!" Quinn chirps, coming to Sammie's rescue, who seems to be rendered speechless. "Sammie here has done an amazing job getting everything organized, down to the smallest details. Isn't that right, Levi?" The tiny, blond woman tilts her head in my direction giving me a pleading look.

I can take a hint. "Absolutely. Everything's going according to plan. Aside from the weather." Aunt Lori laughs as she swats at my shoulder.

"Those meteorologists never can get it right!" Clapping her hands together she says, "Well, I'll head out. I'll see you tonight, Miss Williams." With that, she turns and strolls out of the warehouse, the slam of the door signaling to everyone that she left.

Sammie huffs out a breath before stomping over to the small bathroom, closing the door behind her.

I know my aunt can be... difficult, to say the least. She's constantly running around and getting into everyone's business. Her redeeming quality is that she does it because she genuinely cares. I'm not saying it's right or that people enjoy her meddling, but she's always the first one to reach out a helping hand when she hears someone's struggling. She'll contact every last grandma when she hears someone is in need of a meal. Or the first to send a gift basket to a family who suffered a loss. It's her calling. In this instance though, it's doing more harm than good.

I realize I've been staring at the worn brown door to the bathroom when Quinn stands beside me, nudging me in the stomach with her shoulder. "Aren't you going to go check on her?"

"Me?" I ask, confused. "I think she'd prefer you more than me."

Quinn groans, head thrown back, arms reaching to the sky. "You're an idiot. You've been trying so hard to get her to like you, the moment you have an opportunity it's like you're completely oblivious."

"I should go after her? She's in a closed bathroom, I'm pretty sure she wants to be left alone."

"I'm telling you," she pushes up her glasses, "you need to go check on her." When I don't move, she goes behind me and starts pushing me in the direction of the bathroom.

"Alright, alright. You're one persistent little thing."

"Damn, I mean, darn right." Her cheeks flush pink with her slip-up, but she's adorable.

Dodging through the maze of objects that covers the floor, I reach the door and gently knock. Nothing. I get no response from the other side of the door. "Sammie, are you alright?" Waiting a bit longer, I try again. "Sammie?"

This time I hear a sniffle. Is she crying in there? "Sammie, I'm coming in."

Luckily the door is unlocked. Stepping into the small room, Sammie is standing in front of the mirror, eyes red rimmed. Closing the door behind me to keep everyone from seeing, I slide in behind her and place my hand on her shoulder. We are squeezed in the tiny room between the toilet and the sink, only inches separating us.

"What's going through that pretty head of yours?" My hands slide down her arms and back up to her shoulders, offering comfort. I hate seeing her cry.

Wiping her hand down her face, she sighs. "It's nothing." She looks at my reflection in the mirror as she speaks, her voice quivering.

"Sammie," I say, voice soft, "if you're crying, it's not nothing. Let me help." She closes her eyes, arms bracing on either side of the sink as she lowers her head. One of my hands moves to her back, stroking down the length of her spine. She breathes deeply, her body relaxing.

"Forget it, I'm fine." Suddenly, she pushes herself off the sink, turning to face me.

Our mouths are inches apart and the urge to kiss her is overwhelming. Instead of keeping my hands to myself, they gently rest on her waist. The large, tattered sweater she's wearing hides all those luscious curves that fit my hands perfectly.

It's my turn to breathe deeply as I look into those giant blue eyes still glassy with tears. The pull towards her is consuming me. The tension between us is palpable. Just the thought of the taste of her lips, the soft feel of them against mine has my mouth dropping open and head tilting ever so slightly. Sammie does the same, like the intensity growing between us is drawing us together. Leaning even closer, our lips almost meet before she pushes away and opens the door.

"It's nothing."

Chapter Nine

Sammie

S taying late at the warehouse is about to bite me in the ass. Covered in red paint, I sprint through the apartment door, dodging the various Christmas decorations, and head straight for the shower. There's no way I can show up late to the city council meeting today after what happened with Mrs. Haverford.

There's just something about that woman that gets under my skin. Maybe it's her putting herself into this whole project, or maybe it's the subtle way I feel she's belittling all the work I've done. Every ounce of my energy and passion has gone into creating this masterpiece and she calls it a 'mess'.

Scrubbing away at the stubborn paint on my arms with my luffa, my mind drifts to Levi. The way his eyes glanced between me and his aunt shows that he knew how I would feel about her showing up. Then, the way he followed me to the bathroom...

Levi's presence had been a balm to my raw nerves. His strong hands gripped my shoulders, running down my arms while I tried to compose myself. Then, when his hands rubbed up and down my spine, my body ignited. All my awareness focused on his hands on my body and where I wished they would go. Fighting the urge to touch him, I needed to get out of there. He was just so close. *Damn that tiny bathroom.* I wanted him so badly, but I couldn't. *I can't.* My parting words were more me trying to convince myself than a rejection of him. It *has* to be nothing, but I'm finding my reasoning for why is dwindling.

I normally don't let my emotions get the better of me, but let's blame it on the stress. Every snowflake that's fallen has been a setback to the final preparations that I now only have two days to complete. Yes, we've been able to get almost everything ready for when the weather lets up, but time won't be on our side. Once again, I find myself cursing the lady who vacated this position a month before Christmas.

But then I wouldn't have the job.

Finally spotless, I exit the shower and throw on a long-sleeved emerald wrap dress. Not bothering with a ton of makeup, I swipe some mascara, blush, and lipstick before throwing on knee-high boots and walking out the door.

Traffic on Main Street was slow at this time of night, so I was able to walk in thirty seconds before the meeting began. Thank God.

"Welcome everyone, to the City Council meeting taking place on the twenty-second of December in the year two thousand twenty-two." Mayor Desmond stands at the podium addressing the small crowd and city chairmen. "On tonight's docket, Louise Warner will speak on the state of the city museum and the report from the inspector. Ronald Paulson will discuss the ongoing renovations at the community center. And Miss Samantha Williams will be speaking on the updates to the Christmas Spectacular. Following these scheduled sessions, there will be a time to hear from the community as well on any issues they wish to address."

Looking around the room at all five of us sitting in the audience—three of whom are set to speak—makes me think that time will be short.

Say what you want about small towns, but they put in a lot of effort to keep their towns nice. The city is taking time to renovate old buildings, discuss needed improvements, and then follow through with them. The only reason Louise can speak today is that she brought up concerns about the state of the building the museum is housed in, and the board took her concerns seriously.

Next, Ronald discusses the new additions to the community center. The new flooring was put in this week and by next week everything should be complete.

"Thank you, Ronald, for sharing." Mayor Desmond looks down at the speaking schedule, clearing his throat. "Miss Samantha Williams."

It's so quiet in this room that you could hear a pin drop as I step up to the microphone. Putting on a smile, I greet the council. "Good evening, ladies and gentlemen of the board."

Mr. Brown, a quiet elderly man, leans toward his microphone. "Good evening, Miss Williams. What do you have to report for us this evening?"

"Thank you, Mr. Brown." I strategically keep my eyes away from the far end of the table where Lori Haverford is sitting. My emotions are still too raw from earlier. "The Christmas Spectacular is quickly coming together. We've had to move our work into the warehouse for the time being due to the recent winter weather, but we're hopeful that we can get back outside soon."

"You know, I drive by the town square every day and it's looking a bit lackluster." Christine Mayhew, a middle-aged teacher, and member of the board announces in an accusatory tone.

"Yes," I agree with her because she's not wrong. "It does look underwhelming at the moment, but I can assure you that by Christmas Eve, you will all be blown away. We have a lot that needs to be transported from the warehouse to the town square. It's ready and waiting for the weather."

A voice I was hoping wouldn't pipe up rings out from the end of the table. "I've seen that warehouse and I can attest that there *is* a lot of stuff going on. It makes one wonder if you are capable of giving Rose Prairie the Christmas Spectacular it deserves."

This. Bitch.

Swallowing hard I silently count to ten in an attempt to calm myself before responding. "The warehouse is currently being used as a workspace, so yes there *is* a lot of work going on. But I can assure you, everything is ready. There's no one more dedicated to this than I am."

"Well then," Mayor Desmond cuts in, "it sounds like we'll be seeing a magnificent display come Saturday. Thank you Miss Williams." Bless this man. "Moving right along, the mic is now open for community concerns."

I look down at my boots as I walk back down the aisle to my seat. I was afraid that something like that was going to happen, but I had hoped it wouldn't. Of course, Lori couldn't help herself. It almost makes me think that she wanted the position for herself. Come to think of it, she might have.

The room is filled with awkward silence as we wait for someone—anyone—to approach the microphone. Again, I look at the tiny crowd before me and it appears that no one has anything to add before the meeting is adjourned.

The sound of large boots on the carpet moves down the aisle, and a large back that I know so well walks right past me and straight up to the microphone.

"Good evening, everyone. My name is Levi Ross." His hands are clenched in fists, the whites of his knuckles showing how hard he's squeezing. "I've decided to speak this evening in support of Sammie, Samantha, Williams."

Oh, my god. What is Levi doing here? I didn't hear him come in.

"I've had the privilege of being appointed by this board as the carpenter to assist Sammie with fulfilling her vision for the Christmas Spectacular. I know that this event means a lot to so many people, but no one cares as much as Sammie. She's worked tirelessly to design and create dozens of brand-new attractions for our town's winter festivity." He turns around, brown eyes twinkling as he makes eye contact with me. "I've never seen someone so dedicated and passionate about Christmas."

Tears are threatening to pool in my eyes at his support, but I blink them back. He has no idea how much I needed this.

His voice rings out with conviction. "I think the best decision this board could've made was hiring Sammie. She doesn't need the people that hired her to be doubting her like this. That's all."

Stunned. I'm absolutely stunned. This kind, sweet, handsome man spoke up for me. Not that I needed him to—I'm fully capable of speaking for myself—but no one's stood up for me so publicly before. I wonder what it must have cost him to get in front of his aunt and speak my praise.

Mayor Desmond's voice takes over, yanking me from my thoughts. "Thank you, Mr. Ross. Is there anyone else who would like to speak?"

I can't take my eyes off of Levi as he walks past me and out the doors of city hall.

Chapter Ten

Levi

Uncharacteristic anger sparked through me when those women—my aunt being one of them—judged and doubted Sammie's hard work. I've been with her almost every day for the last three weeks and I couldn't—*wouldn't*—tolerate listening to them speak to her like that.

After seeing Sammie upset earlier, I found that I would do anything I could to keep her from crying again. Whatever it might be to her, this thing between us is far from nothing to me.

Hearing her car door close as she left for the meeting, I found myself grabbing my keys knowing exactly where I would be going. I didn't want her to face the council alone knowing my aunt would most likely bring up her visit from this afternoon.

Now, as I walk out of the door to city hall, my anger is far from sated. She'd stood there and listened to them doubt her abilities and did her best to articulate her point professionally. But as I watched them listen to her, they were completely unmoved.Nothing could have stopped me from walking up to that microphone.

Slamming the truck door, I drive. Anger isn't an emotion that comes easily to me. It takes a lot to get me this worked up and my growing feelings for Sammie and the doubt the council was putting on her stirred that fire.

Without a destination in mind I drive aimlessly around town and down dark backroads until my body relaxes, the anger passing. Glancing at the clock on the dash, I notice I've been driving for an hour. With nowhere left to go, I make a u-turn and head back into town.

It doesn't take long to turn down the street to the duplex, parking next to Sammie's car in the shared driveway before making my way inside. It's been a long day and I have a feeling the next several days will be as well. Readying for a shower, I discard my shoes and peel off my shirt. Just as the button slides through the loop of my jeans there's a knock at the door.

Knowing who would be at the door at this time of night, I debated putting a shirt on. With a smirk, I step through the living room not bothering to button my pants or dawn a shirt.

Let's see her get flustered.

I don't even look through the peephole to make sure Sammie is standing there, I just open it. The look on her face is priceless. Her mouth is poised to speak but freezes the minute she sees my bare chest. Carrying lumber, hammering nails, and sawing through wood have all done their part helping to tone and harden the muscles of my upper body. Sammie's eyes rake down my chest and over the abs my hard work has won me.

Coming to her senses, she closes her mouth and audibly swallows, making a crooked grin cross my face. "Um," she stammers, still flustered. "I came to talk to you."

Crossing my arms over my chest, I take in her appearance. She's no longer wearing that dress that hugged her ass making it hard for me to concentrate during the council meeting. No, she's wearing a full-on Christmas PJ set, her long-sleeved top featuring a Christmas tree, and matching green flannel pants. Her dark hair is tangled in a bun on the top of her head and her face is clean of any makeup.

She looks even more beautiful than ever. The tightening in the crotch of my jeans agrees.

"I assumed so," I say as I lean against the doorjamb. I'm rewarded with her gaze once again traveling down to the top of my unbuttoned jeans and—holy Christ—she bites her lip. What I wouldn't give to know what that feels like. The bite of her teeth against my soft flesh. My spitfire making her mark. It takes every ounce of willpower I have to speak and not groan in frustration. "What did you need to talk about?"

She's still knocked off balance and call me crazy, but I love seeing her flustered. She's always so composed and snarky, but this? This I enjoy. "Um, can I come in?" It's still snowing lightly, and her arms are hugging her body as the cold seeps in.

Stepping back, I motion for her to come inside, closing the door behind her. "Sorry about all the boxes, I haven't had much time to get settled." No time, really. The day after I came into town, I started working with her on the Christmas Spectacular. Boxes are still piled and stacked throughout the apartment, some with opened lids as I've dug through them looking for specific items.

She stops in the middle of the living room, her head turning as she takes the mess. "Sorry, I was going to come over sooner, but you weren't home."

I lean against the island separating the kitchen from the living room, watching her. "What's up?"

71

"Can you put on a shirt or something?" Her eyes widen as I gently shake my head. Clearing her throat, resigned she says, "Well, I wanted to thank you." Sammie looks so fucking beautiful my fists grip the edge of the counter, fighting to not go to her.

My voice comes out deep and straining with longing. "No thanks necessary. They were out of line with how they spoke to you, and I wanted to put them straight."

"No, not for just that," she sighs. "Thank you for showing up for me. I had no idea that you were in the audience until you went up and started speaking. You're just," she pauses. "You're just an amazing person, Levi. Just, thank you." Her shoulders loosen as she exhales, the tension in them dissipating.

I can't take this space between us any longer. Releasing my fists, I walk straight up to Sammie, hand cupping her jaw to tilt her face towards mine. Her sharp inhale at my touch is making my dick harden in my jeans. Leaning in I whisper, "I'll always be there for you, Sammie." No longer fighting the intense connection I feel for her, I lower my lips to hers.

For a moment, she doesn't kiss me back and doubts enter. Maybe she doesn't want me as I want her. Just as I'm about to pull away, Sammie's soft lips press against mine and pure ecstasy washes through me. Her cold hands slide around my hips making me gasp.

"Come on, Levi. Can't handle my cold hands?" She chuckles against my mouth before biting my lower lip.

Good God. Moaning, I slide my tongue into her open mouth. She tastes like nothing I've ever had before. She's the perfect combination of spicy and sweet that sets my blood pumping. One hand slides down her curves before I grab a handful of that ass I like staring at so much. "God, I want you," I growl.

My gorgeous, spitfire of a woman once again knocks me off my feet.

"Then take me."

Chapter Eleven

Sammie

Levi kisses me like he's a starved man. His tongue slips into my mouth, teasing me while his hand grips my ass. The skin of his stomach is warm under my touch, and I pull myself towards him, lessening the space between us. This is what I wanted so badly in that small bathroom. For his lips to be on mine. His body pressed against mine.

His lips move from my mouth to the side of my neck as my breathing speeds up. "I've wanted to kiss this freckle from the moment you stepped out of your car," he murmurs. He flicks his tongue against my neck and my hands travel up from his waist to grip the back of his head. He grips my bun, pulling my head back, giving him more room to explore.

"Don't stop," I manage to breathe. My pulse thrums from his possessive touch, soaking my panties. I can feel his erection through his jeans against my stomach and I grind my body against him, eliciting a deep growl from his throat.

Fuck, that was hot.

Without warning, Levi pulls back before sliding both hands to my ass, picking me up. From this new angle, I wrap my arms around his shoulders, my teeth finding the skin of his neck and gently nibbling at him. The cold of the island jars me as he sets me on the counter, rough hands slipping under my shirt, tickling my sides as he raises it over my head. Free of my shirt, my fingers play with the loose edges of his jeans, running back and forth between the elastic edge of his boxers.

The bra I was wearing is loosened and thrown across the room. Nothing is separating our upper bodies and I press my hard nipples against his chest, the rough sensation making me moan. I want him. So bad. My body is ready for him, needs him. Levi kisses his way down my chest, applying enough pressure to ease my back flat against the counter. Taking a nipple into his mouth, he sucks hard, making my hips grind against him to ease the pounding pulse between my thighs.

"Not yet, spitfire," he croons before moving to my other breast and taking it into his mouth. My legs come up to either side of his chest, hands sliding to cup the back of his head as he licks and sucks his way down my body.

He stops once he reaches the tie of my flannel pants, looking up at me with those dark eyes hooded with desire. He watches my face as he slowly peels my pants and underwear off my body, leaving me naked, stretched before him.

My breathing is hard and ragged. My body is on fire for him. Every beat of my heart has my pussy throbbing, needing his touch. Without wasting a moment, his tongue flicks along my skin until his breath is hot against my cunt, making me squirm in anticipation.

Slowly, so slowly, his tongue glides through my wet center. I let out a moan as his tongue swirls across my sensitive clit making spots dance in my vision.

He feels so good.

He takes his time, savoring my body, making me writhe for him. Tension is building within me with each stroke, each caress of his tongue. My cries and moans grow louder the closer he brings me to ecstasy.

Just as he is about to push me over the edge, my pussy clenching and throbbing, Levi stands.

"What the hell are you doing?" I snap, angry that I was just moments away from orgasm. Sitting up, I watch as Levi removes his pants and boxers and stands before me. His dick is large and throbbing with his need and I am knocked breathless at the sight. Levi catches me looking at him and smirks as he leaves me sitting on his counter and heads to his bathroom.

"You better not leave me like this, Levi. I swear to God." Hearing his chuckle from the hallway, he makes his way into the kitchen, opening the condom in his hand with his teeth. "Thank God."

"I'd never leave you like this Spitfire. Nothing could stop me from seeing you come all over my dick." I watch as he slides the condom over his impressive length and steps toward me. "You ready, beautiful?"

"Stop talking," I demand as I pull his mouth to mine. Rough hands grip my hips, my thighs opening to give him access. He runs his cock along my throbbing pussy, coating himself with my wetness before notching himself at my entrance. Pulling back, my gaze meets his as he slowly sinks himself into me. We both groan at the connection between our bodies, my cunt squeezing around him with growing need.

Leaning back on my hand to give a better angle, Levi thrusts in and out of me, hitting a spot that has me seeing stars. His rough hands pull my hips to meet his hips as his mouth seeks out my nipple. Each touch, every movement has me coming undone. Levi must feel the need to consume me because his thrusts pick up speed, no longer slow and smooth but quick and unrelenting. My breasts bounce as he pounds into me, pushing me higher and higher.

My muscles clench around him, making him hiss as my body rises closer and closer. Unable to form words, moans, and sounds of pleasure leave me as my body seizes in orgasm. My pussy squeezes around his large cock as sensations have my body spasming with pleasure.

"Spitfire," he manages to grunt as he thrust into me, once, twice before he joins me.

• • ᴖᴖ • •

I WAKE UP IN LEVI'S bed, his arm tossed across my naked stomach as he slumbers peacefully next to me. After our session on the counter, Levi carried me to his bathroom where we took a hot shower while we both came down from our orgasms. He took his time, using the soap to massage my muscles, making me relax into him. It wasn't long before we found ourselves back in his bedroom, him deep inside me.

Not wanting to wake him, I gingerly slide out from his hold and tiptoe into the living room. Our apartments mirror each other, and I find myself a bit disoriented as I silently searched for my clothes, still not completely awake. Quickly dressing, I sneak out the door and walk through the frigid cold. The snow has stopped, and the sun is beginning to rise, making the snow shimmer like glitter.

Immediately the thought of last night and what happened with Levi drifts away as a torrent of things to do for the Christmas Spectacular races through my mind. There's so much to be done.

ALL TANGLED UP

Entering my apartment, I hurriedly shower before dressing in warm clothing and heading out to the warehouse. There's no time to waste.

Chapter Twelve

Levi

My phone alarm blares from the nightstand beside the bed. Sitting up, Sammie isn't next to me. Vaguely, I remember waking up at one point with her head on my chest, so I know she slept over. Stabbing the dismiss button on the alarm, I crawl out of bed.

Last night had been unexpected, to say the least. If you would have told me this time yesterday what was going to happen, I wouldn't have believed it. Just to be sure she's not here, I wander down the hall and to the living area. Her clothes are gone, all except her bra which is hanging off the arm of the couch—the same place it landed last night. Glancing out the window, her car is gone as well. Which is when I notice that the sun is out, and the snow is no longer falling.

Smiling to myself, I know exactly where my spitfire went.

With a pep in my step, I walk into Tall, Dark, and Coffee and order drinks for Sammie and myself. I figured she would have wanted to get as early a start as possible and wouldn't have stopped to eat or drink anything. I already stopped at Mama's Cakes and picked up some croissants and a few donuts for breakfast.

Thinking she's at the warehouse loading things up in her car to be transported, I start driving around the town square. Just as I'm about to make a right-hand turn onto Main Street,

I notice someone standing on top of the gazebo and my heart drops to my stomach.

What the hell is she doing?

Slamming on the breaks, thankful that no one is behind me, I pull over before jumping out and running across the square. Sammie somehow got a ladder up and is attempting to string the lights on the snowy roof of the gazebo. Alone.

Frustration bubbles under my skin. Hadn't I told her not to come here without me? What she's doing isn't safe under normal circumstances, but now? The snow hasn't even begun to melt, she has no safety harness on, and no one is here to help her. Rubbing my forehead as I look up at her, I also can't help but admire her tenacity and dedication. She's the only woman I know who'd dare to do anything like this by herself. *My stubborn spitfire.*

Too nervous to call out to let her know I'm here worried I'd startle her; I watch as she meticulously threads the lights to the nails at the top of the cupola—the central junction of the roof— before heading back to the edges. After hooking the lights at the bottom edge of the roof, she looks down and notices me.

A stubborn look crosses her face. "How long have you been watching me?" Small bits of hair have slid free from the beanie she's wearing, framing that gorgeous face of hers.

"Long enough," I call up to her. "I told you next time we'd come out here together. What the hell are you doing Sammie?" I'm more concerned for her safety than angry at this point.

"I don't need your help with this," she fires back. I shake my head. Typical. She wouldn't see the harm in coming out and doing it all herself.

"Oh, sure," I reply, voice dripping with sarcasm. "There's no need for someone to hold the ladder for you. Or to make sure you don't slip and fall. It's perfectly safe."

She smiled, a wicked gleam in her blue eyes. "So you already know. Perfect." This woman, who completely has my heart, is infuriating. She continues to make her way around the roof of the gazebo, securing it at the top point before heading back to the edge.

My eyes never leave her as I follow her on the ground as she works. There's no way I'm going to leave her to fall twenty feet to the ground. Rose Prairie's gazebo is built on a concrete base that raises the structure higher than normal, heightening my worry.

"You don't have to stand there, you know," she teases. "I'm going to be fine. You could make yourself useful and bring a truckload of stuff from the warehouse."

Shaking my head, I reply, "Not a damn chance, Spitfire. I'm staying right here."

"I'd rather you get things set up," she retorts.

"I'm good right here." I smile up at her and see her eyes narrow down at me before she continues to work.

I can hear her muttering to herself as she reaches to loop the lights on the cupola. Just as it hooks, Sammie's feet slip out from under her. "Shit!" she screams, arms flailing.

She slides down the sloped roof, my stomach in knots as she tries to gain purchase on the slick roof. With nothing to hold onto, she slides over the edge.

There's no fucking way I'm going to let her fall. Running forward, I manage to soften her fall just before she hits the ground. My body became the soft spot for her to land, me not quite able to catch her. Both of us fall to the ground, a tangle of limbs, panting and breathless.

Pulling her into my lap, I cradle her to my chest. To think that she could have fallen with no one here to catch her. She could have been left laying in the snow until someone found her. It sends shivers down my spine. Placing a kiss on her beanie-covered head, I ask, "Are you okay?"

Sammie buries her face in the hollow under my chin, breathing heavily. "I think so." Her hands hold tightly to my coat, pulling her closer to me. Running a soothing hand up and down her back, we sit in silence for a moment, clutching onto one another.

"Are you two okay?" A distant voice calls to us. Cara, the owner of Tall, Dark, and Coffee jogs through the snow. "I heard a scream and saw you fall." Sammie untucks herself from my lap as Cara gets closer.

"Yeah, I'm fine," she calls out, climbing from my lap and standing. "I got lucky."

Sammie helps pull me up as Cara comes to a stop in front of us. "You okay, Levi?" I've known Cara since Middle School when her family moved into town. She opened her coffee shop and bookstore after graduating from Rosewood College and I'm happy that she's been successful.

"Me? I'm fine. My heart might have stopped for a moment, but I'm good." Sammie shoots me a quick look before turning back to Cara.

"I'm glad you're both okay. That's a long fall." She looks up at the Gazebo that towers over the square. "Let me know if you need anything." We both thank her as she heads back across the street.

Sammie smacks me against the chest as soon as Cara leaves. "Your heart did not stop, quit being so dramatic."

"Spitfire, my heart came alive the moment I saw that first day. But seeing you on that roof? Yeah, my heart stopped. You scared the shit out of me." Her blue eyes soften at my words, and she caresses my face.

"I guess I'm sorry then," she says just before gently kissing my lips. "Forgive me?"

Wrapping my arms around her, I kiss her back, harder than before. "Forgiven."

"Good." She presses another quick kiss against my lips before shoving me in the chest. "Now, let's get back to work."

Chapter Thirteen

Sammie

I t's here. All my hard work has led me to this moment.

Christmas Eve day has been a whirlwind. Levi and I walked the square one last time hand-in-hand, checking on every aspect of our work. Yesterday, after I fell from the roof of the gazebo, Quinn and some of her friends from Rosewood helped us get all of the materials from the warehouse set up. Levi and his friend Greyson worked to get the sleigh put together since it would have been impossible to transport it once it was secured.

Everything was finally ready.

Staring at my reflection in the mirror in the bathroom, I breathe deeply. *Whatever happens tonight, you did your best.* Tears pool in my eyes and I quickly bat them away. Can't go ruining all the makeup I put on for photos.

The front door opens, the soft creaking of the hinges alerting me. "Sammie? Are you ready?" Sticking my head through the doorway, I watch as Levi heads toward me. He's got on dark jeans and a white cable-knit sweater that has my mouth watering.

Our relationship—if that's what we call it—has fit seamlessly with daily life. For so long, I kept him at arm's length, scared he would work against me when really, he's the best thing that could have happened. He's the most supportive person I've ever met.

Last night, he slept over at my place, the whole time making fun of all the Christmas decorations covering every surface. When I say I love Christmas decorations, it doesn't just mean lights. My apartment looks like a Hallmark movie threw up, and it's exactly the way I like it.

"Just about." My dark blue suede dress falls to my knees, the patch of skin between my knee and boot covered with thick tights. Snow began falling again late afternoon and I couldn't be happier about it. I love snow when it's not ruining carefully laid plans.

Levi stops behind me, wrapping his strong arms around my waist as I put on earrings. "You look beautiful, Spitfire." He leans down kissing his favorite freckle on my neck making me shiver.

"Thanks," I sigh, leaning back into him. "Let's just hope the lights are just as beautiful or else I won't have a job anymore."

He turns me around to face him. "Don't worry. The square has never looked this good for any Christmas Spectacular. Just wait for all the oohs and ahs to slow down before you make them grovel for forgiveness at your feet." He bends down, kissing my lips until I can't think about anything else. Thankfully, he pulls back before I lose all sense as well and jump his bones. Well, bone-er.

Scoffing, I say, "I'd never *make* anyone grovel." A picture of Levi on his knees before me offers a different idea. "However, you can kneel before me anytime." With a wink, I grab my purse and head out the front door.

"Don't tempt me, Spitfire."

.. ✃ ..

"WELCOME TO THE ONE hundred and twelfth annual Rose Prairie Christmas Spectacular!"

From the steps of the Gazebo Mayor Desmond addresses the overflowing crowd of spectators gathered to see the unveiling of the lights. From what I can tell, people have come in from neighboring towns for the celebration. Currently, the only lights on are the streetlamps that ring the square with their lit garland, making for a soft glow. Large snowflakes fall peacefully to the ground as soft Christmas music is played in the background.

"Before we turn on the lights, I wanted to take a moment to acknowledge all the hard work that has gone into making tonight a reality. Miss Samantha Williams! Will you please come up here?"

What? Levi claps animatedly next to me urging me forward. I really don't want to stand in front of all these people, but there's no helping it now. Rolling my eyes, I squeeze my way through the crowd and up the steps next to the mayor.

"Samantha here was appointed in November to undertake this amazing endeavor by the City Council. I can assure you that she has gone above and beyond to make this the grandest Spectacular that any of us have seen." Applause breaks out and I smile at the crowd. When the applause dies, Major Desmond continues. "There is one other person who was instrumental in what you see around you. Levi Ross, if you would please come forward."

Levi weaves through the crowd, jogging up the steps with the cutest grin on his face. He stands next to me, wrapping his arm around my waist as we stand in front of the crowd.

"Levi was the carpenter that came in and helped build the structures you see around you." Heads turn to take in the dark shapes around the square as they applaud.

"Now, without further ado, let's start the countdown!" Starting at ten, the entire crowd yells out a countdown like it's New Year's Eve in Times Square.

"Two, One!" Light engulfs the square and the look of joy that crosses the faces of the people in the crowd brings tears to my eyes. It's everything I've ever wanted. All the hard work, anxiety, and stress were all for this.

My dream has come true.

Levi pulls me in close, kissing my temple. "It's amazing, Spitfire. Absolutely amazing." People are clapping and cheering at the display.

The entire walkway leading up to the gazebo is covered in a tunnel of soft white lights. The Christmas Tree made of lights sparkles and twinkles, already drawing a crowd. I spot a small family walking through the gingerbread houses, their eyes lighting up in fascination.

A flash of a camera has my vision spotting as the local journalist snaps a picture of Levi and me taking in the result of all our hard work.

"C'mon. Let's go see it." Levi guides me down the steps and through the light tunnel. Everything turned out just as I had envisioned. The wonder and magic of Christmas have taken over Rose Prairie and my heart feels full.

ALL TANGLED UP

Children are dragging their parents to Santa's Sleigh, which has a line for the photographer, and some people are dropping donations into the bucket instead of getting their picture taken. Their generosity makes my heart soar. College students are laughing and making faces through the Mr. and Mrs. Claus cut outs, and families are enamored with the gingerbread house, their smiles conveying excitement.

After we walk through the displays, we make our way around to the stands to enjoy some hot chocolate and sweets. Everything has gone off without a hitch. Cara's hot chocolate is amazing and the chocolate truffles from Mama's Cakes are mouthwatering. We taste and cast our votes for the Chili Cook Off, laughing and joking the entire time.

Everything with Levi comes so easily. In the beginning, I tried so hard to keep him away, but his happy nature started to wear me down the minute I stepped out of my car that first morning. He's the most kind and supportive person I've ever met. Sure, I still get annoyed at him, but it's never for long. He makes me feel like myself—I don't have to hide anything. I'm completely comfortable with him. This thing between us is new and undefined but I can't help but picture a life here in Rose Prairie with him.

Levi pulls me close, our bodies pressed together. "Mind if I go and look for my family? I can meet you at the gazebo later."

"Sure. I'll survive," I tease. He places a sweet kiss on my lips before walking away, looking back and smiling at me before he disappears through the crowd.

I'm not alone long before a tiny blond with giant glasses comes barreling at me. Quinn wraps her arms around me, hopping up and down with excitement. "You did it, Sammie!

You fu-freaking did it!" Laughing at her enthusiasm, I hug her back.

"I couldn't have done it without you, Quinn. You worked just as hard as I did."

She shakes her head, her glasses slowly sliding down her nose before pushing them back up. "Nope. No way. You didn't see me up here at the as-butt crack of dawn in the bitter cold putting up lights. All I did was get us more help and paint a couple of things." She shrugs. "No biggie."

"Still, you've been a great help." Quinn's been amazing with all the things she managed to handle. I knew I could focus on decorations with Quinn working behind the scenes.

She waves off my praise. "It was nothing. Anyway, I was heading over to the stands for some treats. Wanna join me?"

"No, thanks. Levi and I already grabbed some." I hold up my steaming cup of hot chocolate in apology. Quinn gives me one last hug before waving goodbye, and once again I'm alone to bask in the joy of the night.

Instead of standing around, I head down the light tunnel to the gazebo. I can sit and people watch while waiting for Levi. Walking towards me wearing a fur-lined coat is Lori Haverford. Gritting my teeth, I fight the urge to turn and walk in the opposite direction, but she's already spotted me.

"Miss Williams!" she calls. "I've been looking all over for you."

Coming to a stop in front of her, I force a smile on my face. "Mrs. Haverford." I nod my head in greeting, but not willing to say more.

"Dear, I wanted to speak to you for a minute." She places a gloved hand on my shoulder nudging me to the side of the walkway. I'm uncomfortable and I don't want to be in this conversation. If she thinks I'm going to stand here and listen to her belittle my hard work, she's got another thing coming.

"I just wanted to say that I'm sorry."

I'm honestly shocked. My eyebrows furrow in my confusion. "Excuse me?"

"I apologize for how I've treated you the last several weeks. I don't like change and there's a lot of that going around recently, and I think I took it out on you." She has a contrite look on her face, making me believe she's being genuine.

"Um, I'm not sure what to say," I admit.

She gives me a kind smile. "You don't have to say anything, dear. I know I didn't show you my best side and I hope that we can get to know one another." She leans in close, waving me in. "Plus, I can see that my nephew thinks very highly of you, and I don't wish to make family dinners awkward."

Chuckling, I find myself smiling back at Lori Haverford. "That would be nice."

Lori beams at me. "Good! Now, let me go and enjoy this magnificent display you've put together. It's truly magical." She pats my arm as she walks away.

This night has gone perfectly. Sitting on the bench in the gazebo, I glance around the square listening to the Christmas music and the laughter. This is what I wanted. This is what Christmas is. Spending time with loved ones, laughing and teasing, and seeing the beauty in ordinary things. Breathing out, I sigh, content.

"Taking in all your hard work?" Levi leans against the frame of the gazebo, watching me. "You look so beautiful." He walks towards me, reaching his hand for mine.

Grasping his hand, he pulls me off the bench before placing a kiss on my lips. It's not a quick, sweet kiss. It's hungry, like he's been wanting to kiss me all night.

Pulling back, I run my hand over his cheek. "You're not too bad yourself," I tease.

Levi leans into my palm before kissing it. "I have something for you." He moves us over to the center of the gazebo. "Look up."

Wrapped in his arms, I tilt my head up to the ceiling. There, hanging from the middle, is mistletoe. "You planned this?" I ask with a chuckle.

"Oh, I hoped for it." Leaning down he kisses me, his tongue sliding into my mouth in a passionate embrace. "I also wanted to say," he adds, breathless from our kiss, "that you are the most amazing person I've ever met. Spending the last three weeks with you, learning how big your heart is, seeing your passion—has made me fall for you." He drags in a deep breath. "This thing between us is new, but I wanted to make it official. You're everything I want, Spitfire." He leans his forehead to mine, his admission barely a whisper.

Tears fall from my eyes for the first time tonight. Of everything this night has to offer, this by far—his admission— has my heart soaring. Voice full of emotion, tears falling, I answer. "Levi, I want to be with you too." Rough thumbs brush away my tears as our lips connect.

I don't know the exact moment when we got all tangled up with one another, but I can say that this is the best Christmas I've ever had.

Epilogue

Christmas Eve
Five Years Later
Levi

"Three, two, one!"

In a flash, the lights of the town square are flipped on but my eyes are on my two favorite people. My wife holds our two year old daughter, Holly, who's blue eyes are round saucers as she looks up at the Christmas lights. Like mother, like daughter.

Sammie and I got married four years ago on this very day, surrounded by the thing that brought us together. My life has become so much more that I thought it would five years ago after moving back to Rose Prairie from the city. Looking back, the pull I felt all that time ago was my heart dragging me to Sammie.

Over the last several years, we've continued to work together on the Christmas Spectacular, adding more attractions—so much so that our little town made national news. We now have people driving and flying in from across the country to experience our town's Christmas Spectacular. It's done wonders for Rose Prairie and our local businesses are booming with orders from all over.

Sammie has worked her magic as the town's event coordinator and has added many new traditions for all times of the year. She's even dragged my aunt into helping her and I'm happy to say that they've warmed up to one another.

"Lights!" Holly's adorable squeal brings a smile to my face. Her chubby little hands reach for the lights strung overhead, fingers grasping.

"Yes, baby," I laugh, "lights." Sammie looks back at me, her face glowing with affection. I kiss my spitfire of a wife before reaching for my daughter. "Let's go look at the lights!"

Placing our toddler on the ground, Sammie and I each grab a hand and lead her through the lights.

Holly is just like her mother, spunky attitude and all. And she's already inherited her mother's love of Christmas.

Thanks For Reading

Thank you for reading *All Tangled Up*.
Originally, I hadn't wanted to write a holiday romance, but when the mood struck, I couldn't shake it! Writing this story was so much fun for me. The dynamic between Sammie and Levi as soon as they were on the page together had me cracking up. (I hope it had you laughing too).
Be on the lookout for more Rose Prairie stories!
If you could, please take a moment to rate and review on Amazon, Goodreads, Instagram, or wherever you post reviews.
As an indie author, ratings and reviews are the best way of getting my work out there for other people to read. A little goes a long way!
Don't forget to follow me on Instagram @authorsierrashipley [1]for more up-to-date information about future books!
Thank you for your support!
Until next time,
Sierra

---

1. https://instagram.com/authorsierrashipley?igshid=YmMyMTA2M2Y=

About the Author

S ierra Shipley is a born and raised Midwest girl. She spends her days with her lovable rescue pup, Trip. Her ideal day is spent drinking coffee, reading, and dreaming.

Sierra has always wanted the romance she's read in books. Pair that with an active imagination and a love of creativity, and you get a writer!

Her goal is to create steamy, romantic stories with characters that people can relate to.